D1385104

This edition published by Parragon Books Ltd in 2017
and distributed by

Parragon Inc.
440 Park Avenue South, 13th Floor
New York, NY 10016
www.parragon.com

ISBN 978-1-4723-7821-7

Printed in China

Things You Never Knew About Santa Claus

Giles
Paley-Phillips
& Rowan
Martin

PaRRagon

Bath • New York • Cologne • Melbourne • Delhi
Hong Kong • Shenzhen • Singapore

Way up in the cold North Pole,
far, far away from you,

Santa Claus is doing things
you won't believe are true!

He does of course have reindeer,
like all the stories say,
but he also has …

Dancer

Blaze

...a dragon that he rides on every day!

One thing we all know
is that Santa loves to eat,
but did you know...

...COLD PIZZA is his favorite midnight treat?

Santa Claus loves bumper cars, and chasing reindeer around.

When he's tired of Jingle Bells,
he likes a

HARD ROCK
SOUND!

Santa likes to dye his hair,
which makes him look quite weird.
Would you believe
his latest look?

A green and purple beard!

On Christmas Eve he goes by sleigh,
but Santa loves to SCOOT!

Then he wears his bright blue shorts
and not his crimson suit.

Sharing gifts all around the world,
He's never lost his way.
But sometimes Santa does get lost—
When he takes some time away!

SANTA'S COMING...

Yes, Santa Claus does lots of things,

it's all COMPLETELY true!
But the thing he likes to do the most ...